# CHEIKH SARR

# Beyond the Whistle
## A Coach's Love Story

DPI

DADYMINDS PUBLISHERS INSIDER

First published by DADYMINDS PUBLISHERS INSIDER 2024

This novel is entirely a work of fiction. The names, characters and incidents portrayed in it are the work of the author's imagination. Any resemblance to actual persons, living or dead, events or localities is entirely coincidental.

Cheikh SARR asserts the moral right to be identified as the author of this work.

Cheikh SARR has no responsibility for the persistence or accuracy of URLs for external or third-party Internet Websites referred to in this publication and does not guarantee that any content on such Websites is, or will remain, accurate or appropriate.

Learn more about the DADYMINDS Company: https://www.dadyminds.com

The Publisher: DPI (DADYMINDS PUBLISHERS INSIDER) is the TM Department in charge of book publishing and author services at DADYMINDS HOLDINGS LLC.

Email: info.dadymindsltd@gmail.com

WhatsApp: +250 (781) 355-361/+1 (307) 323-4616

Mail: 1007 North Orange Street, 4th Floor Suite #2987, Wilmington, Delaware, United States

First edition

ISBN: 979-8-22-484669-6

Editing by Anath Lee Wales

This book was professionally typeset on Reedsy.
Find out more at reedsy.com

*This book is dedicated to everyone, simply open the next pages and allow me to tell you a story like no other you have ever read!*

"Try to see if you can make things work, but if you can't, don't force it. Recognize the incompatibility and consciously decide to stay in spite of it, or to move on because of it."

~(Racco, 2017)

# Contents

# Preface

In the pages that follow, readers embark on a compelling journey through the realms of love, passion, and the intricate tapestry of human relationships. "Beyond the Whistle" unveils a riveting narrative, skillfully crafted by a fresh storyteller, where the echoes of a coach's whistle serve as a prelude to a tale that transcends the boundaries of the ordinary. This fiction invites you into the world of Coach Kazimir, a figure whose life intertwines with the beautiful Mandilé, against the backdrop of the enchanting country of Roshwari. The allure of this narrative lies not only in its portrayal of a love story but also in the nuanced exploration of cultural, religious, and societal intricacies that shape the characters' destinies. As you turn the pages, you'll witness the blossoming of a love that defies conventions and navigates the delicate dance between tradition and personal aspirations.

The red rose, elegantly gracing the cover, becomes more than a symbol—it is a reflection of the profound emotions, the drama, and the enduring passion that weaves this tale together. The author masterfully interlocks the fibres of love and drama, creating a narrative that resonates with readers on a visceral level. Each chapter unfolds as a captivating episode, inviting you to delve into the complexities of relationships, the clash of cultures, and the pursuit of personal fulfilment in the face of societal expectations.

"Beyond the Whistle" stands not merely as a work of fiction but as a mirror reflecting the multifaceted nature of the human experience. Through the lives of Kazimir and Mandilé, the story digs into the complexities of love, the challenges posed by differing beliefs, and the inflexible pursuit of happiness. In these pages, you'll find a captivating fiction that transcends the ordinary, leaving an indelible mark on the reader's heart. "Beyond the Whistle" is more than a story—it is an invitation to explore the complexities of love, to challenge preconceived notions, and to embark on a journey where the human spirit triumphs against the backdrop of cultural diversity.

So, dear reader, let the whistle's call beckon you into a world where love knows no boundaries, and the drama unfolds with every turn of the page. "Beyond the Whistle" awaits, promising an immersive and thought-provoking experience that lingers long after the final chapter.

# Acknowledgement

...Dedicated to those and all those who, despite the tests of loyalty and gratitude, taught me the invaluable lessons of discernment and resilience.

Mamadou, pocket money is not only for Tacos

Awa, you won't be in every book, you might skip one or 2. You are the definition of, euuuuh ok chose just two words to replace your name for the publications: love, perseverance, patience, kindness, generosity.

Throughout my entire coaching and teaching career, I have met great people, great coaches and teachers, and great human beings, who cleared my paths to a purposeful life.

- If you taught me at school, this book is for you, thank you, I got educated.
- If you instructed me at the university, this book is yours, thank you, I have gained humility.
- If you dragged me toward the sports fields, thank you, I love my job.
- If you have been annoyed, this book is for you, thank you, I have learned about boredom.
- If you loved me, this book is for you, thank you, I discovered the meaning of being alone

Thanks to you Anath Lee WALES, for being here when I needed it the most. Your *professionalism and bits of advice make it easier for this work to be released.*

*Thank you to my mentor, coach Ado SANO, with whom, in 1993, I heard for the first time John Wooden's name. I realize today that was the beginning of a passion for basketball that will never end.*

*Thank you to Coach Gora MBAYE: you taught me how to play the game and be a good student. I hated you when you kicked me out of the court for the entire season for me to focus to my senior high school exam. I realize today how your decision impacted my life, both academically and professionally.*

*A million thanks to the most pleasant people I have ever met, especially during the past 3 years.*

*This book is for Tony, Lily, Sony, Nezy, and Jovy, you guys have been genuine, reminding me that "what goes around, comes around". But remember, Eve was kicked out of heaven because of eating an apple, you should make the reverse trip because of eating chocolate.*

*To those daemons who taught me the meaning of hanging out: Yves, Luc, Dave. Stay Sneaky*

*To Moyiz, Djiby and Delph, worth filling up my emergency contacts list.*

*"If you are scared of confronting people who made you angry, please do not punish innocent people. Suffer alone".*

# Prologue

~⚬⚭⚬~

Rainer Martens[1], one of the most prolific American scientists in the field of coaching and kinesiology has proven there is the possibility to combine coaching and teaching careers. One of his books, "Successful Coaching" (Martens, 2004), has given hope to many sports coaches who aspire to build a successful team or help athletes grow and succeed simply by following Martens' principles of coaching and teaching. It might be simple to see it that way knowing that coaching is a very demanding and high-pressure profession. For many years, I have been following this path and

---

[1] "Rainer Martens, PhD, has coached at the youth, high school, and collegiate levels and has studied sport as a research scientist. The founder and president of Human Kinetics, he also started the American Sport Education Program, a leading coaching education program for many years. Recognized as a pioneer in the development of sport psychology, Rainer is the author of more than 80 scholarly articles and 18 books. He has been a featured speaker at over 100 conferences around the world and has conducted more than 150 workshops and clinics for coaches and athletes at all levels. After receiving his PhD in physical education from the University of Illinois at Champaign-Urbana in 1968, Martens was a member of its faculty for 16 years. A past president of the National Academy of Kinesiology, he has been recognized for his contribution to sport by the National Recreation and Park Association and by his induction into the National Association for Sport and Physical Education Hall of Fame. He has received Distinguished Alumni awards from Hutchinson High School, Emporia State University in Kansas (where he earned a bachelor's degree), the University of Montana (where he earned a master's degree), and the University of Illinois".(Human Kinetics, 2024)

never found a way to escape. Many times, I have been facing complex and emotionally charged situations without looking for an opportunity to meet an advisor (a coach) or psychologist who can provide an external and objective perspective, helping me see challenges more clearly and make informed decisions.

From my own experience, I can disclose that coaching can be emotionally taxing, especially when dealing with burnout, family issues, travelling and the stress of competition. I have seen the need for a confidential space to express my feelings, receive support, and develop coping strategies. Then, from my previous and first book, written months ago, "*Sport Psychology and Performance, in Africa*", I found out that writing can be a therapeutic and constructive outlet to release the pressures of life. Despite the opportunities to self-reflect, express emotions, learn and grow, writing, especially fictional storytelling like "*Beyond the Whistle*" provides me with a safe space to explore feelings through narrative and characters. It allows me to temporarily detach from the pressures of coaching, offering a mental retreat into a world of my creation.

I did not seek advice from a mental specialist or psychologist, (I could have), instead, the writing process and the stories, align with the theme that describes the struggles of a peer, who is facing precariousness, distress, love against all odds, family issues and tough decision, serve as teaching tools where metaphors and allegories in the narrative convey valuable lessons and insights for both the potential readers and myself.

Nevertheless, writing Kazimir's story, despite the fictional aspect of the story, can be realistic and I believe, the challenges he faced are very common and very people-centred. This makes me point the finger at how crucial it is for sports coaches to have their psychologist or advisor maintain their mental well-being, enhance performance, prevent burnout, and navigate the complex challenges associated with coaching.

It's an investment in their development and a proactive step toward long-term success and satisfaction in their coaching career.

This story is a warning, a call to those coaches, and I believe there are many Kazimir around us, who need to escape a moment and find a way to release the pressure of life.

# Introduction

In the complicated needlepoint of life, where the echoes of victories on the soccer field reverberate far beyond the boundaries of the field, emerges a tale of love that defied the norms and transcended societal expectations. *"Beyond the Whistle: A Coach's Love Story"* invites you into the captivating world of Kazimir, a seasoned soccer coach, whose journey unfolds against the background of triumphs, challenges, and a forbidden love that would reshape his destiny.

Between the cheers of victory and the weight of defeat, Kazimir found himself at a crossroads, seeking comfort in the enchanting land of Roshwari. As he embarked on a coaching role for Roshwari's national team, he could not have foreseen the profound impact this decision would have on his personal narrative. Leaving behind his wife, Saran, and their son, Rashid[2], in Sangouna, Kazimir set forth on a path that would lead him to Mandilé, a Christian waitress at Ping Coffee Shop, and into the intricate dance of forbidden love.

The age-old clash of cultures, the societal whispers, and the complexities of relationships wove a tale that extended beyond the boundaries of the soccer field. Mandilé 's firm determination, supported by her sister Linassa, and

---

[2]  The rightly-guided

friends Sandra, Saline, and neighbor Clara, became an encouragement of hope in a love story that defied all odds. As Kazimir's coaching career rose, the shadows of societal expectations intensified. Mandilé, grappling with the challenges of a significant age difference and a desire for independence, found herself at a crossroads. Secrets unfolded, friendships were tested, and in the midst of societal turbulence, the trio of Kazimir, Mandilé, and Sandra discovered the enduring strength of love, friendship, and the human spirit.

"Beyond the Whistle" is a narrative that explores the transformative power of love, the resilience required to defy societal norms, and the intricate dance of relationships that go beyond the victories and defeats on the soccer field. Join us on this emotional journey where love, in all its complexity, emerges victorious, proving that sometimes, the most profound victories lie beyond the whistle's call.

# Chapter I: The Final Whistle

## The collapse and flow of democracy in Sangouna

Since gaining independence in 1960, Sangouna was initially conceived as a democratic example, mirroring the aspirations of many African nations in the post-colonial era. However, the political trajectory deviated over the years, echoing a common theme across the continent. Leaders, once chosen through democratic processes, found it difficult to relinquish power, and the ideals of justice, equity, and compassion became casualties of political self-preservation. In contrast to some African nations where leaders garnered recognition for supporting the principles of justice and compassion, Sangouna diverged from this trajectory. The past five years have witnessed a significant decline in stability as the government, sensing a threat from a popular opponent exposing corruption and mismanagement, responded with a heavy hand. The political climate became fraught with tension, leading to the imprisonment of thousands and the forced exile of those who dared to voice dissent.

Sangouna, once hailed for its democratic experiment, is now grappling with the consequences of suppressing opposition voices. The incarceration of thousands and the creation of political refugees cast a shadow over the democratic aspirations that once defined the nation. The youth, burdened by economic hardship and disillusioned by the erosion of democratic principles, have lost hope. In search of a better future, many have resorted to the perilous journey across the ocean, viewing immigration as their only means of escaping the shackles of poverty and political oppression. In this tumultuous context, Kazimir finds himself and his family navigating the complex and challenging landscape of Sangouna. The nation, once celebrated for its democratic ideals, now stands at a crossroads where the erosion of hope and the pursuit of a stable future are intertwined with the broader narrative of a democratic experiment gone awry.

## A story of disorganization and insecurity

The Sangouna National Team, despite its illustrious past and successful record, stands as a paradox within the realm of soccer. While the trophy cabinet echoes tales of past glories, the team's current state reveals a landscape of disorganization and a palpable absence of cohesive leadership. Several years removed from their last title triumph, the Sangouna National Team finds itself in the agony of a prolonged decline. The echoes of that previous victory have gradually faded, replaced by a sense of urgency and an unrelenting desire to reclaim former glory. The team's disarray becomes evident in its on-field performance and the off-field dynamics that shape its existence. At the helm of this tumultuous journey is the team president, a figure marked by profound insecurities and a low threshold for effective leadership. Their sole focus lies in reclaiming the title, creating an environment where winning trumps all other considerations. In the pursuit of victory, the president's approach lacks the nuance of acknowledging the importance of performance, teamwork, and the hard work that underpins sustained success.

The team's recruitment of Coach Kazimir becomes a symbolic attempt to inject new life into a stagnant system. Kazimir, known for his coaching prowess, is entrusted with the daunting task of steering the team back to its former glory. However, the inherent disorganization and the president's fixation on winning at any cost create a challenging backdrop for Kazimir's endeavours. Despite his best efforts, Kazimir faces the impossible challenge of navigating a team culture that prioritizes immediate success over the long-term building of a cohesive and resilient squad. The president's relentless pursuit of victory, coupled with a lack of respect for the principles of performance and hard work, sets the stage for a clash of ideologies that hinders the team's progress. In this turbulent narrative of sportsmanship, the Sangouna National Team becomes a reflection of the pitfalls that arise when organizational disarray and insecure leadership overshadow the pursuit of excellence. The team's struggle for success becomes a complex tapestry, woven with frustration, unmet expectations, and a longing for the days when victory was not just a destination but a byproduct of a well-organized and harmonious collective effort.

After the final, Kazimir stood on the sidelines, his heart pounding with anticipation. The Sangouna National team had fought valiantly, but the final whistle blew, signalling their defeat against an undefeated African team. The disappointment was palpable, and Kazimir, known for his past successes, faced the bitter taste of failure. As the news of his dismissal reached him, he couldn't help but feel a mix of emotions — disappointment, regret, and a gnawing desire for redemption. With his coaching career at a crossroads, Kazimir pondered the next move that would define his professional and personal trajectory.

In the quiet of his office, Kazimir revisited the highs and lows of his tenure with Sangouna. He couldn't shake off the feeling that there was more to accomplish, a legacy yet to be forged. It was in this reflective moment that he stumbled upon a coaching opportunity in Roshwari, a country known for its pristine landscapes and a soccer culture that beckoned him. The decision was made; Kazimir would embark on a journey to Roshwari, leaving behind the familiarity of Sangouna, a decision that would shape the chapters of his life in ways he could never have anticipated.

# An example of success and integrity in soccer coaching

Coach Kazimir stands as a model of success and dedication in the realm of soccer coaching, a luminary whose journey through the corridors of education and experience has left an indelible mark on the field. After graduating from the prestigious University of Madifé in the west of Sangouna with a degree in sports sciences, Kazimir's trajectory in the world of soccer is defined by a relentless pursuit of knowledge, opportunities seized, and a commitment to excellence. Kazimir's academic journey became a foundation upon which his coaching prowess would flourish.

Having climbed the entire spectrum of degrees a soccer coach could acquire, his academic resume shines with achievements that reflect not only intelligence and knowledge but also an insatiable thirst for continuous learning. His educational pursuits took him beyond borders, to the hallowed halls of institutions in Asia and Canada, where he honed his skills and gained a global perspective in the intricate field of sports sciences. Ambition courses through Kazimir's veins, a driving force that propels him to strive for greatness in every facet of his coaching career.

The experiences garnered on international soil have not only broadened his tactical acumen but have also imbued him with a cultural sensitivity that enriches his approach to coaching. Kazimir, with a wealth of knowledge at his disposal, stands at the forefront of the soccer coaching landscape, a testament to the heights that ambition and diligence can achieve.

Beyond his undeniable success, Kazimir is characterized by a profound sense of responsibility and integrity. A man of conscious choices, he sees soccer coaching not just as a profession but as a calling to uplift the sport and the individuals under his guidance. His willingness to extend a helping hand to others, be it players or fellow coaches, reflects a generosity of spirit that transcends the boundaries of competition. However, beneath Kazimir's amiable demeanour lies an unwavering stance against behaviours of disrespect and indolence. His coaching philosophy is rooted in the belief that success is not only measured by victories on the field but also by the values instilled in the athletes under his charge. Kazimir rejects shortcuts and quick fixes, championing a path of discipline, hard work, and unwavering respect for the sport and its participants. In the complex textile of soccer coaching, Coach Kazimir emerges as an inspiration of intelligence, ambition, responsibility, and respect. His story is one of continuous ascension, marked by a dedication to the craft and an unyielding commitment to fostering a culture of excellence in the beautiful game.

# Kazimir's insecurity and unfulfilled potential

Coach Kazimir, an experienced wise man with a wealth of soccer expertise, finds himself entangled in the complex trap of insecurity and unsteady professional ground. Despite his dedication and earnest efforts to elevate the Sangouna National Team, the lack of a sports agent and the absence of a secure contract cast a pending shadow over his tenure. As the whistle blows on Kazimir's coaching journey, a disconcerting sense of insecurity takes root. The very arena he dedicated his expertise to now reveals the harsh realities of a sports landscape where the absence of proper representation and contractual stability can swiftly unravel even the most promising coaching careers.

The feeling that courses through Kazimir's veins is one of frustration and unfulfilled potential. His dismissal becomes a poignant reminder that the world of sports, while celebrated for its triumphs, can be unforgiving in its treatment of those without the protective shield of a sports agent. The lack of an advocate leaves Kazimir vulnerable to the capricious whims of organizational decisions, often driven by factors beyond his control.

The absence of a secure contract amplifies Kazimir's sense of insecurity. In a profession where stability is as elusive as the next championship, the uncertainty of contractual terms magnifies the precariousness of coaching careers. Kazimir, despite his tactical prowess and commitment, becomes a casualty of a system that fails to provide the necessary support and safeguards for coaches navigating the tumultuous world of sports. As Kazimir contemplates his departure from the Sangouna National Team, there lingers a palpable mix of disappointment and the lingering question of what could have been. The potential that once thrived on the training ground, the strategic brilliance that could have reshaped the team's fortunes, is abruptly cut short, a casualty of a system that demands resilience yet withholds the necessary assurances. In the recesses of Coach Kazimir's mind, there brews a potent blend of determination and the sobering realization that, in the absence of adequate representation and contractual security, even the most skilled coaches can find themselves on the periphery of the very arena they sought to conquer.

# Chapter II: The Decisions

## Kazimir's friends and extended family: a source of advice

Kazimir has planned before talking to his wife Saran to engage with his extended family and friends in the social media discussion groups to seek their bits of advice regarding the potential move to Roshwari. He finds himself in a more grounded and reassuring state. Some specific insights or advice resonated with him because many of them shared their positive experiences with moving to Roshwari. They emphasized the welcoming nature of the people, the opportunities for personal and professional growth, and the overall positive atmosphere in the country. It's heartening to know that others have successfully navigated this journey.

In the family and friends group chats, valid concerns were raised, particularly about adapting to a new culture and being away from his family. However, the shared practical tips and advice on overcoming these challenges have been immensely helpful for him. He believes that with proper preparation and a positive mindset, he can tackle these issues.

He feels a sense of reassurance and optimism. The shared experiences and advice have provided a valuable perspective, making the prospect of moving to Roshwari seem less daunting. He is not only considering career opportunities but also embracing the idea of immersing himself in a new culture. It sounds like the collective insights have been a guiding light for him. He believes he can make a more informed decision, leaning towards the excitement of embracing a new chapter in his life, with the support and shared experiences of his extended family and friends serving as a foundation for his decision-making process.

It's now time to face his wife to talk about it in order to see if thoughtful bits of advice from friends and family will match her viewpoint. He wishes from the bottom of his heart that Saran will embrace an openness and a thoughtful approach to making a decision. He wishes that, together, they will navigate this journey with the wisdom and support of those who care about us. The only decision that matters the most for Kazimir is the one he will get after discussing it with his wife Saran.

# Touchline

3

Late at night, Kazimir shared the news with Saran; the air in their living room felt heavy with uncertainty. The prospect of a move to Roshwari, while promising, meant a separation from his wife and young son, Rashid. Saran, understanding the gravity of the decision, encouraged Kazimir to seize the opportunity. Rashid, oblivious to the intricacies of his father's career, sensed a shift in the family dynamics. Kazimir grappled with the guilt of leaving his loved ones behind, yet the allure of Roshwari and the potential for redemption fueled his resolve.

---

3   The touchlines are the two long lines running the length of the soccer field and are placed at an equal distance from each other on either side. They define the boundary of the field of play and show the inbounds area where the ball must stay throughout the match. Here, it symbolizes the boundaries in which every decision should be taken with the family.

Coach Kazimir and his wife Saran sit on the couch, surrounded by an air of anticipation. The room is dimly lit, and a map of Roshwari is spread out on the coffee table.

Kazimir
(leaning forward)
"Saran, I've been offered the coaching position in Roshwari. It's a significant opportunity for my career."

SARAN
(nods)
"I know, Kazimir. It's an incredible chance for you, and I'm proud of what you've achieved. But you know my job here in the government is crucial, and I can't just pick up and move."

Kazimir
(smiles)
"I understand, Saran. I've been thinking about it a lot. It won't be easy, but I believe we can make it work."

SARAN
(worried)
"It's not just about us, Kazimir. We have Rashid to think about, his school, and his friends."

Kazimir
(seriously)
"I've thought about that too. Roshwari offers excellent schools, and Rashid can adapt. Besides, it's an opportunity for him to experience a different culture."

SARAN
(nods)
"True, but what about us? We'll be apart for a while, and long-distance relationships are challenging."

Kazimir
(softly)
"Saran, we've always faced challenges together. This is just another hurdle. I'll come back whenever I can, and we can use

technology to stay connected."

SARAN
(sighs)
"It's just hard, Kazimir. I'll miss you, and Rashid needs his
father around."

Kazimir
(places his hand on hers)
"I'll miss both of you too, but this is an opportunity we can't
pass up. We've always supported each other's dreams, and I believe
this will bring us even closer when we overcome it."

SARAN
(smiles)
"You're right. We've faced challenges before, and we've always
come out stronger. Let's do it. Let's make this work."

They share a tender moment, acknowledging the difficulties ahead
but confident in their ability to navigate them together.


The plane touched down in Roshwari, and Kazimir was greeted by a wave of warmth from the locals. The soccer community welcomed him with open arms, and the prospect of coaching the national team fueled his passion. The picturesque landscapes of Roshwari, with its vibrant culture and clean, organized surroundings, provided a stark contrast to the challenges he faced in Sangouna. Yet, in this new beginning, Kazimir couldn't shake off the sense of longing for his family, thousands of miles away. The decision to leave Saran and Rashid behind was a heavy burden, one that would shape the emotional landscape of his days in Roshwari.

Coach Kazimir's arrival at the Roshwari National Team Federation is met with an air of anticipation and curiosity. The team's performance has been decent, but the hunger for improvement and a desire to ascend to greater heights permeate the room. The meeting is a crucial juncture, where goals and expectations will be outlined for the next four years under Kazimir's leadership.

# Roshwari National Soccer Federation Meeting room

The meeting room is decorated with the colours of the Roshwari flag. Coach Kazimir sits at the front, facing the members of the Roshwari National Soccer Federation (RONASOFE). The room buzzes with a mixture of excitement and a palpable enthusiasm for change.

After a quick introduction of each RONASOFE member and welcoming talks, the president Jimmy TRECA allowed the newly appointed coach to talk.

```
Kazimir
(energetically)
"Good morning, everyone! I'm honoured to be here, and I'm excited
about the journey ahead. I've had the chance to observe the team's
performance, and I see tremendous potential."

The members of the Federation nod, acknowledging Kazimir's
presence and words.

Kazimir
(smiles)
"Our goal is clear: to elevate the Roshwari National Team to new
heights over the next four years. We might be at a decent level
now, but I see immense room for improvement. Together, we'll work
towards creating a team that not only competes but dominates on
the international stage."

PRISCILLA, federation member #1
(raising hand)
"What specific goals do you have in mind, Coach Kazimir?"

Kazimir
(leaning forward)
"First and foremost, we aim to qualify for the major international
```

tournaments consistently. That means putting in the work during
qualifications and showcasing our prowess on the field. I believe
we can make Roshwari a formidable force in the soccer world."

ZACKARY, federation member #2
(nods)
"And what about player development?"

Kazimir
(smiles)
"Thanks, this is a great question. Let me remind you that player
development is at the core of our strategy. We'll invest in
nurturing young talent, refining skills, and creating a cohesive
team. The youth system will be a priority, ensuring a pipeline of
skilled players ready to represent Roshwari."

PAUTY, federation member #3
(leaning forward)
"What about our coaching staff? Are any changes planned?"

Kazimir
(confidently)
"We'll assess the current staff and bring in experts where needed.
A strong coaching team is crucial for our success. We'll also
focus on sports science, fitness, and mental conditioning to
ensure our players are at their peak."

HUREKIM, federation member #4
(raising hand)
"How do you plan to engage with the community?"

Kazimir
(enthusiastically)
"Community engagement is vital. We'll initiate grassroots
programs, connect with local schools, and inspire the next
generation. The support of the community is a powerful force, and
we want Roshwari to rally behind its national team."

The meeting continues with discussions about tactical approaches, scouting,
and fostering a culture of discipline and teamwork. Coach Kazimir's vision

sets the tone for an era of transformation and growth for the Roshwari National Team. The room echoes with a renewed sense of purpose, as the federation members and Kazimir embark on a collective journey to elevate Roshwari's soccer standing over the next four years.

# Chapter III: A New Chapter in Roshwari

## Roshwari, the land where soccer unites and nature thrives

Roshwari, a small yet vibrant country with a population of 12 million, is nestled in a picturesque landscape that seamlessly blends natural beauty with the fervour of soccer. The nation has embarked on a unique journey of using soccer as a powerful tool to mend ethnic divergences from its past, while also leveraging the richness of its natural resources to foster economic development and tourism. The majority of Roshwarians, about 60%, are Roman Catholic, with another 13% Protestant. Only about 2% of the population is Muslim. About a fourth of Roshwarians are adherents of indigenous beliefs. However, these numbers and divisions are not clear-cut. Roshwarians share cultural values especially social cohesion, resilience, and hard work among others, with *"Roshiwanga"* being the common language, spoken in all parts of the country. Other official languages are English and Hindi.

Soccer is more than just a sport in Roshwari, is a cultural phenomenon. The nation's passionate love for the game transcends ethnic boundaries, bringing people together on the fields, in stadiums, and during spirited celebrations. Soccer serves as a common language that unites diverse communities, fostering a sense of national identity and pride. Roshwari has faced historical challenges with ethnic divergences, but soccer has become a means of healing and reconciliation. The sport provides a platform for communities to come together, celebrate shared victories, and build bridges over historical divides. Soccer leagues and tournaments serve as avenues for fostering understanding and unity among the various ethnic groups. Recognizing the economic potential of soccer, Roshwari has strategically invested in the development of the sport. Soccer academies, infrastructure, and youth programs have not only contributed to the nation's athletic prowess but have also become sources of economic growth. The thriving soccer industry attracts sponsorships, investments, and global attention, creating jobs and boosting the economy.

Roshwari boasts a diverse and breathtaking natural landscape, from lush forests and pristine lakes to majestic mountains. The country has capitalized on its natural beauty to attract tourism. Natural zoos showcasing indigenous wildlife, picturesque hiking trails, and eco-friendly resorts provide visitors with an immersive experience, allowing them to connect with Roshwari's rich biodiversity. Soccer tournaments, matches, and events draw international visitors, contributing to Roshwari's tourism sector. The country's commitment to sustainable tourism, combined with the allure of soccer, has made it a unique destination. Visitors can enjoy not only thrilling soccer matches but also immerse themselves in the tranquillity of nature, creating a holistic travel experience. Roshwari's emphasis on soccer and nature as cultural assets has led to increased cultural exchange. International teams, fans, and tourists engage with Roshwari's traditions, cuisine, and hospitality, fostering a global community that appreciates the nation's unique blend of sports and natural wonders.

Some studies investigate the impact of football (soccer) on social cohesion. They have shown how participation in football-related activities contributes to community building, social integration, and the creation of a shared identity among diverse groups (Wicker, Breuer, & Schröder, 2016). In Roshwari, soccer isn't just a game; it's a catalyst for unity, healing, and economic prosperity. The nation's commitment to preserving its natural treasures while leveraging them for sustainable development exemplifies a harmonious blend of sports, nature, and cultural diversity.

It's in this perspective that Roshwari embraced Kazimir with open arms. The soccer community was eager for fresh leadership, and Kazimir's reputation preceded him. As he delved into coaching the national team, the vibrant energy of Roshwari's soccer culture breathed new life into his coaching philosophy. The team responded with enthusiasm, and Kazimir found solace on the field. However, despite the successes on the pitch, a void lingered in his heart. The separation from Saran and Rashid cast a shadow over the victories, reminding him that success, though sweet, was incomplete without his family by his side. Off the field, Kazimir explored the wonders of Roshwari — its bustling markets, serene landscapes, and the cultural richness that surrounded him. Yet, in these moments of admiration, he couldn't help but imagine sharing these experiences with Saran and Rashid. As he settled into his new life, the chapter of his journey in Roshwari extended with a dichotomy of professional achievement and personal nostalgia. The beauty of Roshwari became a bittersweet backdrop to the narrative of love and separation.

## Settling In

In the bustling city of Galida, Coach Kazimir found himself navigating the challenges of settling into a new environment. The transition from hotel living to a more permanent residence proved to be a significant undertaking. Eager to establish a stable base, Kazimir embarked on the task of renting an apartment and securing transportation, only to encounter unexpected hurdles. The realization hit him when he delved into the local real estate market. The high cost of renting an apartment in the city took him by surprise, with figures exceeding his initial budget. Navigating the process with real estate agencies proved to be a labyrinth of paperwork and intricate negotiations. Kazimir, accustomed to the more straightforward procedures in his previous locales, found himself grappling with the complexities of the Roshwari housing market. Undiscouraged, Coach Kazimir persevered in his search for a suitable residence. The real estate agents, however, seemed to wield a considerable degree of influence, making the process more challenging than anticipated. Despite the hurdles, Kazimir's determination remained unwavering as he sought a living space that would serve as a comfortable haven amidst the rigours of coaching the national team.

The challenges extended beyond securing shelter to the realm of transportation. Renting a car proved to be another financial jolt, with rates exceeding Kazimir's initial estimates. The surprises kept coming as he navigated the intricacies of vehicle rental agencies, leading him to reassess and recalibrate his budget to accommodate the higher-than-expected costs. In the end, despite the initial hurdles, Coach Kazimir managed to secure both an apartment (around 16000 Rands) and a car (11000 Rands). The experiences, though daunting, became valuable lessons in adapting to the unique dynamics of Roshwari's living conditions. As he settled into his new residence at 23 Street, Martin Whine, Galida City, Kazimir was reminded that the journey to elevate the national team extended beyond the soccer field, encompassing the day-to-day challenges of building a life in a foreign city.

No matter where or how he lives, Kazimir believes that feeling *at home* always summarizes the same factors: security, comfort, big handfuls of belonging and ownership, lots of fun and success, and a healthy spoon of privacy.

# Kazimir's residence

Located at 23rd Street Martin Whine, Galida City, Roshwari, Kazimir's apartment exudes an air of refined sophistication, a carefully curated space that seamlessly blends comfort with modern aesthetics. Nestled within a prestigious building, the two-bedroom suite stands as a testament to Kazimir's discerning taste and appreciation for the finer things in life.

Upon entering, a grand foyer welcomes guests with a tasteful blend of warm tones and ambient lighting. The walls adorned with captivating artwork provide a glimpse into Kazimir's appreciation for culture and aesthetics. The spacious living room unfolds with plush, inviting furniture arranged in a manner that encourages both relaxation and socialization. Large windows offer panoramic views of the city, allowing natural light to illuminate the room's elegant furnishings. A state-of-the-art entertainment system complements the room, inviting guests to unwind in style.

Adjacent to the living room is a stylish dining area, featuring a sleek table surrounded by comfortable chairs. The ambience is perfect for intimate dinners or gatherings with friends. The open layout seamlessly connects the dining space with the living area, fostering a sense of fluidity. The modern kitchen is a culinary haven equipped with the latest appliances and amenities. Gleaming countertops, high-end cabinetry, and a functional layout cater to both the art of cooking and the joy of entertaining. It's a space where Kazimir's passion for good food and hospitality come together seamlessly.

Each of the 2 bedrooms in the suite is a sanctuary of comfort. Lavish furnishings, including a king-sized bed in the master bedroom, promise restful nights. Thoughtfully designed décor elements and ambient lighting create an atmosphere of tranquillity and luxury. The en-suite bathrooms are a symphony of marble and porcelain, offering a spa-like experience. Luxurious fixtures, a soaking tub, and a spacious walk-in shower complete the picture, transforming the act of self-care into an indulgent ritual. Throughout the apartment, personal touches reveal Kazimir's unique character. Artefacts from his travels, tasteful decorations, and a carefully curated book collection reflect a life rich in experiences and cultural appreciation.

Coach Kazimir, settled into his new apartment, decides to engage in a conversation with his landlord, Mrs. ROSA, a well-spoken and affable local.

Kazimir
(knocking on Mrs. ROSA's door)
"Good afternoon, Mrs. Rosa. I hope I'm not disturbing you."

Mrs. ROSA
(smiles)
"Not at all, Coach Kazimir. Come on in. What can I do for you?"

Kazimir enters Mrs ROSA's office, and they sit in the cosy living room overlooking the beautiful scene of Galida.

Kazimir
(settling in)
"I've been marvelling at the beauty of Roshwari since I arrived. The landscapes are stunning, and the security is top-notch. It seems like a paradise."

Mrs. ROSA
(nods)
"Indeed, we take great pride in maintaining a secure and picturesque environment for our residents. It's essential for the well-being of the community."

Kazimir (serious)
"I've also noticed a stark contrast. The environment is pristine, but I've heard whispers about resource disparities leading to challenges for some residents."

Mrs. ROSA
(sighs)
"You're perceptive, Coach. Despite our efforts, we do face challenges. The economic disparities create imbalances in resource distribution. It puts many low-income individuals, both men and women, in precarious situations."

Kazimir

(concerned)
"How does this impact the community, Mrs. Rosa?"

Mrs. ROSA
(leaning forward)
"Well, the unequal sharing of resources, especially for those with limited means, can lead to vulnerability. Some find themselves in situations where they compromise their values due to economic hardship."

KAZIMIR
(nods)
"It's disheartening to hear. Is there anything being done to address these issues?"

Mrs. ROSA
(Serious)
"Efforts are underway, but it's a complex challenge. We're working on community projects and educational initiatives to empower everyone. But change takes time, Coach."

Kazimir
(resolute)
"I appreciate your honesty, Mrs. Rosa. As a newcomer, I want to understand and contribute positively to the community. Let me know if there's any way I can get involved."

Mrs. ROSA
(smiles)
"That's a commendable attitude, Coach Kazimir. Your presence and willingness to engage speak volumes. We'll welcome any positive contribution you can make."

The two continue their conversation, laying the groundwork for potential collaboration to address the socio-economic challenges faced by the community's less privileged members.

# Chapter IV: Mandilé, Sandra

## A vision of beauty

At the age of 22, Mandilé embodies a captivating vision of beauty, seamlessly blending grace, strength, and the rich essence of African heritage. Standing at a moderate height, her silhouette exudes a natural elegance that catches the eye. Mandilé's features are a celebration of African diversity, with a light skin tone that radiates a warm, golden glow reminiscent of the sun-kissed landscapes of her homeland. Her face, adorned with high cheekbones and a softly defined jawline, tells a story of ancestral beauty. Mandilé's eyes, the windows to her soul, are a hypnotic shade of brown that goes with intelligence, warmth, and a hint of damage. They reflect a depth of emotions, from the joyous highs to the contemplative lows, revealing the resilience within her spirit.

Mandilé's hair, a crown of pride and individuality, frames her face in intricate patterns. Whether styled in braids, curls, or left to cascade freely, her hair is a celebration of cultural richness and personal expression. The strands, catching the sunlight, create a halo of luminosity around her. Her slender yet athletic physique is a testament to her youthful vitality and the strength cultivated through life's experiences. Mandilé moves with a confident and purposeful stride, exuding an undeniable magnetic allure that captivates those around her.

Fashion would be an extension of Mandilé's vibrant personality. Whether draped in traditional African fabrics that tell stories of heritage or adorned in modern, chic ensembles that showcase her contemporary style, Mandilé effortlessly navigates the intersection of tradition and modernity. Her wardrobe is a kaleidoscope of colors, patterns, and textures, mirroring the vivacity of her spirit. In every step, Mandilé emanates a natural charisma that extends beyond physical beauty. It is a charisma born from a depth of character, resilience in the face of challenges, and an unwavering determination to forge her path in a world where love and individuality reign supreme. Mandilé, at 22, is not just a vision of beauty; she is a living testament to the enduring strength and grace found within the hearts of African women.

## Navigating loss, support, and educational challenges

Mandilé's story unfolds against the backdrop of Roshwari, a place where the pursuit of education and the challenges that follow graduation become defining chapters in one's life. Her narrative is a tapestry woven with threads of loss, family support, and the formidable hurdles of securing higher education in a society where individuals bear the weight of their academic aspirations. At the tender age of 17, Mandilé faced the harsh reality of loss when her father passed away. The departure of a parental figure marked a profound turning point, introducing her to the complexities of grief and resilience. In the midst of this emotional storm, Mandilé found solace in the unwavering support of her family – a single mother determined to anchor her children's dreams, a sister named Linassa whose presence became a source of strength, and a military brother named Tad, standing tall as a guardian.

Throughout her high school years, Mandilé navigated the challenges of adolescence with the guiding light of familial love. The pillars of support around her laid a foundation of resilience that would prove invaluable in the years to come. The loss of her father, though a heart-wrenching experience, became a catalyst for Mandilé to forge ahead with determination, honoring his memory through her pursuit of education. The first seismic shift in Mandilé's journey came with her high school graduation.

As the familiar halls of academia gave way to the uncertainties of the future, Roshwari's societal norms cast a shadow on the path ahead. In this society, the responsibility for post-high school education falls squarely on the shoulders of the individual. There are no guarantees, no safety nets; one must either find gainful employment or secure robust financial support to continue their education.

For Mandilé, the realization that her academic journey would face a critical juncture became a sobering moment. The support system that had guided her through loss and adolescence now faced the challenge of aiding her in navigating the daunting landscape of higher education in Roshwari. The absence of a predetermined trajectory heightened the stakes, placing Mandilé at the crossroads of her future.

In this pivotal period, Mandilé's story becomes a reflection of the broader societal challenges. The burden of self-reliance looms large, and the pursuit of education emerges as a high-stakes endeavor. Mandilé, armed with the resilience instilled by her family, stands at the threshold of a journey that will test not only her academic mettle but also her ability to navigate a world where the pursuit of knowledge is a privilege that must be fiercely earned.

## Sandra, a resilient soul

Sandra, a spirited young woman with a radiant personality, embodies a vivacious spirit that refuses to be dimmed by life's challenges. As a black and curvaceous beauty, she navigates the world with a bold and unapologetic confidence. Her dark skin is a canvas that radiates strength, resilience, and a certain magnetic allure that draws people into her orbit. With a penchant for parties and a love for socializing, Sandra is often the life of any gathering. Her laughter echoes with unrestrained joy, a testament to her ability to find moments of lightness even in the face of adversity. Dressed in vibrant, curve-hugging ensembles, Sandra carries herself with an air of self-assurance that demands attention.

However, behind the exuberant facade lies a woman who has weathered the storms of heartbreak. Sandra has faced the sting of rejection, having been dumped by a married boyfriend. Despite the pain, she wears her emotional scars with resilience, turning heartbreak into a source of empowerment. Sandra's approach to relationships is pragmatic, shaped by a practical understanding of the challenges life throws her way. Unfazed by societal norms, she navigates the intricate dance of dating with an unconventional perspective. Her lack of fear in dating friends' boyfriends is not rooted in malice, but rather in a survival instinct driven by a need for essential resources. In a world where financial stability is a constant struggle, Sandra's resourcefulness becomes a defining trait. She navigates relationships strategically, unapologetically seeking companionship that can provide not just emotional support but also tangible assistance in acquiring household products, groceries, and the means to pay her school fees.

Sandra's journey unfolds as a testament to the resilience of the human spirit. Behind the party-loving exterior is a woman who faces life's challenges head-on, finding unconventional paths to carve out a future filled with empowerment and self-sufficiency. In the vibrant tapestry of Mandilé's world, Sandra stands as a dynamic force, a friend whose unyielding spirit adds depth and complexity to the unfolding narrative.

Nevertheless, Sandra's complex relationship with Christianity is a juxta-position of faith and a pragmatic approach to life. Despite identifying as a Christian, her behavior, particularly in her romantic relationships, may seem to lack traditional boundaries. However, for Sandra, this is not a contradiction; rather, it's a survival strategy in the face of life's challenges.

Sandra sees her faith as a source of strength, guidance, and hope. She turns to Christian principles for solace during difficult times and seeks comfort in the teachings of love, forgiveness, and redemption. Yet, her practical side manifests in her willingness to navigate unconventional paths in her romantic life.

Her experiences may have shaped a perspective where survival in a challenging environment takes precedence over adhering to societal norms. Sandra might perceive relationships as a means to access resources, support, and stability. In doing so, she rationalizes her actions within the framework of her faith, believing that God's love and understanding extend to her struggles and choices.

Sandra's story reflects the complexities of navigating faith and pragmatism in the context of personal relationships. Her character adds layers to the narrative, prompting readers to contemplate the intersection of faith, survival, and the pursuit of stability in the face of life's adversities.

# Chapter V: Ping Coffee Shop

~~~~~~~~~~~~~~~~~~~~~~~~

## A glimpse into Mandilé's struggle

Nestled on a nondescript road of 24$^{th}$ Oran Twist Street at Galida, Ping Coffee Shop stands as a modest establishment, its façade hinting at the daily struggles and silent battles waged within its walls. Ping stands for noise because of the horns and motorbike beeping and clanging constantly to warn or call clients on the side of the road. The Oran Twist Street is always busy because the events' venue is on the other side of the road. Ping Coffee Shop's exterior, adorned with fading paint and a weathered sign, reflects the financial challenges that have become synonymous with this low-standing business.

As one steps inside, the air is thick with the aroma of brewing coffee, a stark contrast to the palpable tension that lingers within. The interior, dimly lit and furnished with worn-out tables and chairs, tells a tale of financial constraints that have left little room for aesthetic considerations. The atmosphere is laden with a sense of resignation, a feeling that permeates the very essence of Ping Coffee Shop.

The boss, a figure of authority wrapped in a cloud of questionable ethics, presides over the establishment with an air of indifference. The employees, including Mandilé, navigate their duties under the screen of a less-than-ideal work environment. The boss's treatment of the staff is far from equitable; the unequal power dynamics often lead to exploitation, with attempts to take advantage of vulnerable waitresses.

## A simple espresso mix-up.

In the heart of Galida, Kazimir discovered Ping Coffee Shop, a quaint establishment that would become a haven for contemplation and unexpected encounters. It was here that he met Mandilé, the "Christian waitress"[4] with an infectious smile and a spirit that matched the vibrancy of Roshwari itself. Mandilé's warmth and genuine curiosity about Kazimir's journey in Roshwari created an instant connection. Their exchanges evolved beyond the typical customer-server dynamic, transcending cultural differences and sparking an unforeseen bond.

This is how everything has started.

---

[4]  IStatus acquired from family tradition, not from conviction or faith.

The aroma of freshly brewed coffee fills the air as Mandilé, the vibrant waitress, moves gracefully between tables, taking orders with her warm smile. Kazimir enters, his attention immediately captured by Mandilé's beauty.

```
Kazimir
(approaching the counter)
"Hello. I'll have a seat by the window, please."

MANDILÉ
(smiling)
"Of course, right this way."

Kazimir follows Mandilé to a regular table by the window. He
watches as she hands him a menu.

MANDILÉ
(cheerfully)
"Here you go. Take your time to decide, and I'll be back in a
moment."
```

Kazimir scans the menu but finds himself more captivated by Mandilé's presence than the coffee options. When Mandilé returns, ready to take his order, he's momentarily lost in her eyes.

Kazimir
(nervously)
"I'll have... um, an espresso, please."

Mandilé raises an eyebrow, amused by the unexpected choice.

MANDILÉ
(smiling)
"An espresso it is. Anything else?"

Kazimir
(chuckling)
"Actually, I meant to order a Black Americano, but I guess espresso works too."

MANDILÉ
(laughing)
"Mixing up your coffee orders, huh? No worries; I'll make sure it's the best espresso you've ever had."

Mandilé walks away to prepare the order, but Kazimir can't help but smile at his momentary lapse. When she returns with the espresso, their eyes meet, and there's a playful spark between them.

MANDILÉ
(handing him the espresso)
"Here you go. Enjoy!"

Kazimir
(smiling)
"Thank you. And for the record, I blame your charm for the coffee mix-up."

MANDILÉ
(teasingly)

"My charm? Well, I can't argue with that."


Their banter continues, and as they talk, the connection between
them deepens. Kazimir, now more composed, takes the opportunity.

Kazimir
(smiling)
"You know, I think this espresso mix-up might be the best mistake
I've made in a while. Can I convince you to join me for a cup
sometime when you're not working?"

MANDILÉ
(smiling back)
"I'd like that. Here, let me give you my number."

They exchange phone numbers, sealing the beginning of a connection
sparked by a simple espresso mix-up.

MANDILÉ
(texting)
"Looking forward to that coffee date."

Kazimir
(texting back)
"Me too, Mandilé. Until then."

As Mandilé served coffee with grace, Kazimir found himself drawn to more than the aroma of freshly brewed beans. Mandilé, too, sensed an inexplicable connection that defied the norms of casual acquaintanceship. The brewing romance, however, carried a complexity that went beyond the realms of soccer victories. Kazimir's heart, torn between the love he left behind and the unexpected connection unfolding in Roshwari, faced a dilemma that would shape the subsequent chapters of his life.

# Kazimir, a life changer

Coach Kazimir, deeply influenced by his blossoming relationship with Mandilé, became a loyal customer of Ping Coffee Shop. What started as casual visits for breakfast soon extended to lunch and dinner, marking Ping as more than just a dining spot but a comforting haven. Despite having a chef at home, the allure of Ping's warm ambience and Mandilé's welcoming presence drew him in regularly. Beyond being a customer, Kazimir's genuine nature led him to form connections with the other waitresses. When financial constraints burdened his favourite spot, Kazimir quietly stepped in, offering assistance to the waitstaff in need, not out of obligation but as a testament to his compassionate character. His commitment to the well-being of Ping Coffee Shop extended beyond financial support. When the coffee machine faced an unfortunate breakdown, Kazimir didn't hesitate to contribute to its replacement, showcasing his inclination to contribute to the community he valued. His actions weren't fueled by an attempt to win Mandilé's favour but rather by an authentic desire to support those around him. Coach Kazimir's presence at Ping Coffee Shop became symbolic of his genuine connection with people, reflecting a generosity of spirit that extended beyond the confines of his personal relationships.

Ping Coffee Shop evolved into a pivotal space for Coach Kazimir and Mandilé, fostering not just their love but also serving as a backdrop for cultural exchange. Mandilé, recognizing the importance of integration and understanding, promised to teach Kazimir *"Roshiwanga"*, the intricate language of Roshwari. The afternoons at Ping Coffee Shop transformed into language sessions, with Mandilé patiently guiding Kazimir through the nuances of pronunciation and grammar. These language lessons, held just before Mandilé headed to Galida University classes, became more than a linguistic endeavour. They symbolized Mandilé's commitment to Kazimir's immersion into Roshwari culture and the wider community.

Kazimir, in turn, actively participated not only by learning the language but also by shouldering the financial responsibilities of Mandilé's education. As he generously paid for her school fees and other necessities, the dynamic at Ping Coffee Shop became a beautiful exchange of knowledge, love, and support, showcasing the harmonious blend of their individual strengths in building a shared future. The coffee shop, once a simple meeting place, had transformed into a space where cultural understanding and shared dreams flourished.

However, as they got closer every day, Mandilé couldn't hold her feelings about the work environment and decided to share her concerns with Kazimir. She made him understand that he wouldn't be surprised if I got fired or resigned these days because she couldn't support anymore the authoritarian behaviour of her boss asking to be nice to the clients and dress in a skirt. Mandilé is a resilient young woman with dreams extending beyond the confines of Ping Coffee Shop, who grapples with the harsh reality of low wages and an unscrupulous boss. The meagre salary of 1282 rands ($70,00) a mere pittance, barely sustains her daily needs, let alone her aspirations for education. Ping Coffee Shop becomes a microcosm of a broader societal issue – a place where the lack of opportunities forces individuals to endure substandard conditions, where exploitation is reluctantly accepted as the norm.

The precariousness of Mandilé's situation becomes painfully evident when she refuses to succumb to the boss's attempts to take advantage of her. In a society shackled by limited opportunities, Mandilé's courage to stand against exploitation becomes an act of defiance. However, her principled stance comes at a cost – the loss of her job. The firing of Mandilé, a symbol of resilience, further underscores the systemic challenges faced by many Roshwarians women. In the shadow of Ping Coffee Shop, Mandilé's story unfolds as a poignant narrative of strength and sacrifice, a reflection of the harsh realities endured by those caught in the clutches of limited opportunities and exploitative work environments.

Coach Kazimir, witnessing Mandilé's resilience and determination, decided to support her venture into entrepreneurship after her unfortunate dismissal from her previous job. Mandilé, displaying a profound understanding of the market and leveraging her expertise as a master's student in economics, envisioned the creation of *Hot Nuts and Beans Ltd*, a wholesale coffee enterprise. Recognizing Mandilé's business acumen, Kazimir became an instrumental figure in realizing her entrepreneurial dreams.

Understanding the importance of effective communication in business, Mandilé sought the collaboration of her friend Sandra, a public relations student at the University of Galida. Together, they formed a formidable team, Sandra handling the public relations aspect while Mandilé managed the economic dimensions. This collaboration not only showcased Mandilé's commitment to creating a successful business but also highlighted her capacity to build strong partnerships. As the business flourished under Mandilé's strategic guidance and Sandra's adept public relations skills, Mandilé found a newfound sense of financial independence.

Kazimir's support not only alleviated the initial challenges of starting a business but also allowed Mandilé to explore her entrepreneurial spirit, marking a significant chapter in their journey together. The creation of *Hot Nuts and Beans Ltd* became a testament to Mandilé's resilience, her academic prowess, and the unwavering support she received from Coach Kazimir, ultimately contributing to their shared vision of a prosperous future.

## Navigating differences

As Kazimir and Mandilé's connection deepened, the age difference between them became a subtle undercurrent in their relationship. Mandilé, grappling with societal expectations and the disapproving whispers around their age gap, found herself in moments of contemplation. Her friends, Sandra, Saline, and Clara, noticed the internal struggle she was facing.

Simultaneously, Mandilé's desire for independence collided with Kazimir's more traditional values. Kazimir, almost 30 years her senior, often found himself torn between supporting Mandilé's need for freedom and the societal expectations dictating a more conservative approach to relationships. This clash of perspectives introduced a layer of complexity, challenging both Kazimir and Mandilé to navigate through the nuances of their evolving connection.

In Kazimir's apartment at night (away for a minute to bring drink and snacks), Mandilé sits on the couch, visibly conflicted. Saline and Clara, her close friends, have come over to offer support.

MANDILÉ
(looking pensive)
"Guys, I'm really struggling with this. Kazimir is an amazing man, but the age difference... I don't know."

SALINE
(leaning in)
"Mandilé, love doesn't come with an age limit. Look at the way he treats you, the respect, the care. Age is just a number, girl."

CLARA
(nodding)
"Saline's right. Besides, he's successful, caring, and can provide for you in ways that matter. Not everyone finds that."

MANDILÉ
(biting her lip)
"But what will people say? It's almost a 30-year age gap."

SALINE
(rolls eyes)
"Who cares about what people say? This is about you and Kazimir. Age gaps might raise eyebrows, but it doesn't define the love you two share."

CLARA

(smiling)
"And let's be real, Mandilé, you adore him. Your eyes light up when you talk about him. Don't let societal norms dictate your happiness."

MANDILÉ
(sighs)
"I just fear the judgment and the challenges we might face."

KAZIMIR (OFFSCREEN)
(walks in)
"What challenges are we talking about?"

Kazimir enters, sensing the tension. Mandilé looks up, surprised.

MANDILÉ
(stammering)
"Well, um, just some concerns about, you know, the age difference."

KAZIMIR
(smiles)
"Age is just a number, Mandilé. What matters is what we feel for each other. Don't let anything or anyone dim our connection."

SALINE
(nudges Mandilé)
"See, Mandilé? Listen to the man. He's got the wisdom."

CLARA
(grinning)
"And the charm."

Kazimir takes Mandilé's hand, reassuringly.

KAZIMIR
"I care about you, Mandilé. Let's face whatever challenges come our way together."

The atmosphere lightens as Mandilé looks at Kazimir with a mixture of gratitude and love.

```
MANDILÉ
(smiling)
"Alright then. Age be damned. Let's face whatever comes our way."
```

They share a group hug, symbolizing the strength of their bond amidst societal expectations.

After she accepted and clearly understood that the age gap doesn't matter, Mandilé's actions showcase a profound respect for the diversity of beliefs within their relationship. By actively accommodating and participating in Kazimir's religious practices, she creates an inclusive and supportive environment that fosters understanding and mutual respect.

Mandilé's respect for Kazimir's Muslim beliefs is evident in the thoughtful and considerate gestures she extends during his fasting periods. Her actions not only reflect her understanding of Kazimir's religious practices but also demonstrate a deep regard for his personal convictions.

Mandilé recognizes the significance of personal space during fasting periods. She refrains from getting too close and is mindful of Kazimir's comfort level, acknowledging the spiritual importance of this time. Always wearing modesty in clothing. Understanding the principles of modesty within Islamic beliefs, Mandilé ensures that her attire aligns with Kazimir's religious values. She wears modest and decent clothing, showcasing her respect for his faith.

She even actively participates in the breaking of the fast (Iftar), providing Kazimir with foods that adhere to the dietary guidelines observed during Ramadan. Her involvement reflects her support and consideration for his religious practices. Knowing that coffee holds cultural and social significance during the fasting period, Mandilé takes the initiative to help Kazimir brew coffee. This not only aligns with traditional customs but also showcases her willingness to engage in and support his cultural practices.

Mandilé's inquiries about the difficulty of fasting and her encouragement demonstrate a genuine interest in Kazimir's experiences. She actively engages in conversations about his religious practices, fostering an environment of understanding and support. She consistently encourages Kazimir throughout the fasting period, acknowledging the challenges he may face. Her support extends beyond mere acknowledgement, emphasizing her commitment to understanding and respecting his journey. Nevertheless, she has a lot of questions left without answers. She wanted to open a conversation on that difficult religion topic.

MANDILÉ
"Kazimir, can we talk about something important?"

KAZIMIR
"Of course, Mandilé. What's on your mind?"

MANDILÉ
"It's about religion. You know, I've been thinking a lot about our future, and I'm curious about what our kids would follow."

KAZIMIR
"That's a significant topic. What's on your mind?"

MANDILÉ
"Well, I was raised in a Christian family, and you follow Islam. I respect both, and I want our kids to have the freedom to choose. But, I'm a bit confused about what we should introduce them to. What if they ask?"

KAZIMIR
"I understand your concern. It's crucial for them to have the freedom to choose their path. I believe we can introduce them to both our traditions, and share the values, stories, and practices. Let them experience the beauty of both Christianity and Islam."

MANDILÉ
"But what if they ask which one is right?"

KAZIMIR
"Mandilé, the beauty of faith lies in personal conviction. I think
we should encourage them to explore, learn, and make their
decisions when they're ready. We can be there to guide them and
answer their questions, but ultimately, the choice should be
theirs."

MANDILÉ
"So, you're suggesting we expose them to both religions and let
them decide when they're older?"

KAZIMIR
"Exactly. Let them experience the richness of our respective
traditions. When the time comes, they'll make a choice that
resonates with their hearts. It's about understanding, respect,
and allowing them the freedom to shape their spiritual journey."

MANDILÉ
"I appreciate your flexibility, Kazimir. I want our kids to grow
up with the best of both worlds."

KAZIMIR
"And they will, Mandilé. Our home will be a place where they find
love, understanding, and the freedom to choose their own paths."

**But Mandilé envisages the perspectives where kids don't want their
parents' religion or any other.**

MANDILÉ
"Kazimir, what if our kids grow up and decide they don't want to
follow either of our religions?"

KAZIMIR
"Mandy, that's a possibility we need to be open to. It's their
personal journey, and if they choose a different path or decide
not to follow any specific religion, we should respect that."

MANDILÉ

"But how do we handle it? Our families might have expectations."

KAZIMIR
"True, it might be challenging, but our priority is our children's happiness and authenticity. We can explain to our families that our kids have the right to make their own choices. It's about fostering an environment where they feel supported, regardless of the direction their spiritual journey takes."

MANDILÉ
"I worry about judgment from others."

Kazimir
"Mandy, people will always have opinions. What matters most is that our kids feel loved and accepted for who they are. If they choose a different path, we'll navigate it together as a family."

MANDILÉ
"I appreciate your understanding, Kazimir. I want our kids to have the freedom to be themselves."

KAZIMIR
"And they will. Our love and support will be the foundation they need to confidently navigate their beliefs. It's about embracing their uniqueness and allowing them the freedom to shape their own identities."

MANDILÉ
"Thank you, Kazimir. I feel more at ease knowing we can approach this with openness and acceptance."

KAZIMIR
"We're in this together, Mandilé. No matter what paths our children choose, our love and support will be unwavering."

Mandilé and Kazimir found their parents as believers. They did not choose their own religion but it was imposed by their parents. Let's follow their discussion to see where they stand when it comes to choosing a religion for their kids or they will let them decide themselves.

MANDILÉ
"Kazimir, as we delve into the conversation about religion, I
can't help but reflect on how our parents imposed their beliefs on
us without giving us the choice to decide."

KAZIMIR
"It's true, Mandy. We were born into our respective religions
without the freedom to choose. It makes me ponder whether we
should break this cycle with our own children."

MANDILÉ
"I don't want to force any specific belief on our kids, Kazimir. I
want them to have the choice we never had."

KAZIMIR
"I completely agree. But it's not just about avoiding imposition;
it's about creating an environment where they can explore and form
their own beliefs organically."

MANDILÉ
"Do you think we should let them decide when they're older, or
should we introduce them to both our parents' religions and let
them choose from there?"

KAZIMIR
"It's a delicate balance. We can expose them to the cultural and
traditional aspects of both our backgrounds, but the emphasis
should be on letting them explore without the pressure to conform."

MANDILÉ
"I worry about judgment from our families."

KAZIMIR
"It's a valid concern, Mandy. But our priority should be the
well-being and happiness of our children. We can explain our
perspective to our families and hope they understand."

MANDILÉ

"I want our kids to grow up in an environment where they feel free to discover their own spiritual paths without feeling constrained."

KAZIMIR
"Then, Mandy, let's commit to providing them with the freedom to choose, guiding them with love and support as they navigate their own beliefs."

MANDILÉ
"I appreciate your understanding, Kazimir. It's important to break the cycle and allow our kids the autonomy we didn't have."

KAZIMIR
"We're shaping a different narrative, Mandilé--one that values choice, understanding, and respect for individual beliefs."

# Chapter VI: Forbidden Love

⟨ornament⟩

As the whispers about the age difference intensified, Mandilé found herself at a crossroads. The allure of a carefree social life, coupled with Kazimir's occasional absences due to coaching commitments, fueled a desire for independence within Mandilé. Her inclination to spend time with male friends, seeking connections beyond societal confines, created a rift that cast shadows on her relationship with Kazimir.

Undiscovered to Mandilé, Kazimir and Sandra found support in each other's company during moments of Mandilé's social explorations. In a misguided attempt to shield Mandilé from potential judgments, Kazimir and Sandra chose to keep their growing friendship a secret. The clandestine meetings and whispered conversations, however innocent, planted seeds of doubt in Mandilé's heart.

## The unravelling secrecy

The discovery of the concealed friendship between Kazimir and Sandra sent shockwaves through Mandilé's world. The revelation, though innocent in nature, fueled a storm of emotions. Mandilé, feeling betrayed and deceived, confronted Kazimir and Sandra. The simmering tensions boiled over as Mandilé, hurt and angered by the secrecy, contemplated ending both her relationship with Kazimir and her friendship with Sandra. Sandra is the only friend she shares with her ups and downs. She even helped her during the very precarious time, their family are bonded and very tied and they share a business. This situation has emotionally stricken Mandilé's trust in friendship very hard, she felt it was a betrayal.

Kazimir and Sandra expected a fierce reaction from Mandilé because betrayal can have a profound impact on a relationship, leading to feelings of anger, hurt, and distrust. It can come in many forms, such as infidelity, lying, breaking promises, or revealing private information. The one Mandilé is confronting is disloyalty. Betrayal's effects put her in a morbid preoccupation, almost damaging her self-esteem; she felt like losing value and self-doubting. She adopted a retreat mode for a couple of weeks, avoiding socialising with them. Feeling betrayed led her to a sense of isolation, withdrawing herself from others; she found it difficult to share the pain, and she lost trusting new connections. Even at *Hot Nuts and Beans Ltd.'s* office, she will make sure her schedule won't match, doing her best to avoid giving Sandra the opportunity to discuss.

It's in the midst of the chaos that Kazimir and Sandra, realizing the unintended consequences of their secrecy, attempt to explain the nature of their friendship. Mandilé, torn between the desire to save her relationship and salvage her friendship, faced a pivotal decision. In a moment of clarity, she recognized the genuine intentions behind Kazimir and Sandra's actions.

## Forgiveness for love and friendship

Determined to rebuild trust, Mandilé chose to navigate through the complexities and save both her love with Kazimir and her friendship with Sandra.

Mandilé and Sandra sit in the office at Hot Nuts and Beans Ltd, the air tense with unspoken words. Mandilé has just discovered a secret plan between Sandra and Kazimir.

MANDILÉ
(serious)
"Sandra, we need to talk. I know about the plan."

SANDRA
(looking nervous)
"What plan?"

MANDILÉ
(raises an eyebrow)
"The plan you and Kazimir had. I found out."

Sandra shifts uncomfortably, realizing Mandilé is onto their secret.

SANDRA
(trying to deflect)
"Oh, Mandilé, it's not what you think."

MANDILÉ
(cutting her off)
"Don't play games, Sandra. I saw the messages. What were you both thinking?"

SANDRA
(sighs)
"Look, Mandilé, nothing actually happened between Kazimir and me. It was just a moment of confusion, and I deeply regret it."

Mandilé's eyes narrow, clearly hurt.

MANDILÉ
(confused and hurt)
"Why would you even entertain such an idea? Especially with Kazimir?"

SANDRA
(looking remorseful)

"I messed up, Mandilé. I let a moment of weakness cloud my judgment. But I swear, nothing happened, and I value our friendship too much to jeopardize it."

MANDILÉ
(angry)
"This is a betrayal, Sandra. I trusted you, and you were scheming behind my back with Kazimir."

SANDRA
(teary-eyed)
"I know, Mandilé, and I'm so sorry. It was a stupid mistake, and I promise you, it won't happen again. Our friendship means everything to me."

Mandilé takes a moment, visibly torn between anger and the history she shares with Sandra.

MANDILÉ
(softening)
"Sandra, I need you to understand how much this hurts. But if you're sincere about not letting it happen again, we can work through this."

SANDRA
(nods)
"I swear, Mandilé. I'll do whatever it takes to make things right. I messed up, and I don't want to lose you as a friend."

Mandilé sighs, the weight of the situation apparent on her face.

MANDILÉ
"We have a lot to rebuild, Sandra. Don't make me regret giving you a second chance."

They sit in a heavy silence, the future of their friendship hanging in the balance

*"Mistakes are always forgivable if one has the courage to admit them"*

(Srivastava, 2020)[5]

It's very hard sometimes to forgive, especially when holding on to the grudge, thinking it will somehow punish the other person so we can feel good, or hoping we will be protected from getting hurt again; some people don't want to forgive because they believe that fairness and justice must be served since the other person was wrong.

> *"There are occasions when people go through injustice, get setbacks in life, get betrayed by someone they trust. Do not get the response they expect from someone – someone very close, when in need. They attach with themselves the severance, make the mockery a keepsake and try to lead a long life with these- without making any effort to get rid of the swindle. It hurts- gives pain- keeps people stuck- and slows down the momentum of life. There is a way out, forgive, and move on. Forgiveness gives support in leaving behind the matter and quick healing. To lead an everyday life after some point in time, one needs to move towards forgiveness. It prevents one's bitter past from infecting his present and future". (Zafar, 2020)*

However, Mandilé may never understand why Sandra did behave that way. But she understood that forgiveness requires her to look at her anger and pain and choose to let it go. She steps into the process of developing some understanding of Sandra's behaviour and the circumstances. One of the reasons she will forgive is her legendary empathy and compassion. But her primary motivation to let it go remains her sense of goodwill, her benevolence and her compassion toward Sandra. Therefore, her concern for Sandra's welfare as a fellow human being overpowers the hurt generated by the interpersonal transgression.

---

[5] One of the most famous is Bruce Lee's quotes. It demonstrates the ideas of self-effacement, liability, and progress. With these ethical stands, people may lead better lives by accepting their flaws while seeing missteps not as failures but as good on the path to mastery and self-improvement.

It will be constructive for Mandilé to practice forgiveness because it comes with powerful health benefits. Some studies suggest that forgiveness is associated with lower levels of depression, anxiety, and hostility; reduced substance abuse[6], higher self-esteem; and greater life satisfaction.

Nevertheless, Mahatma Gandhi affirms that

*"The weak can never forgive. Forgiveness is an attribute of the strong."*

(Srivastava, 2020)

---

[6] The relationship between the two disorders is bi-directional, meaning that people who misuse substances are more likely to suffer from depression, and vice versa. People who are depressed may drink or use drugs to lift their mood or escape from feelings of guilt or despair.

# Chapter VII: Love against all odds

*~ oⁱgoⁱⱽ ~*

I
n the years that followed, Kazimir's coaching career in Roshwari soared to new heights. The national team, under his guidance, achieved remarkable success, yet the personal challenges persisted. The couple's love story unfolded against the backdrop of victories on the field and societal whispers of it. Kazimir and Mandilé became a symbol of resilience, challenging the norms that sought to dictate the course of their love.

## Mandilé's stress and pressure: the weight of soccer success

As the national soccer team, guided by Kazimir's coaching prowess, steps onto the field, Mandilé finds herself engulfed in a whirlwind of stress and pressure. The success of the team carries significant implications for both Kazimir's professional tenure in Roshwari and the future of their relationship. Mandilé grapples with a complex mix of emotions, each tied to the performance on the soccer field.

She watches the game with bated breath, her eyes fixed on the players moving across the field. Every goal, every save, and every strategic manoeuvre elicit a surge of hope within her. The anticipation of victory fuels her desire for Kazimir to achieve success on the pitch.

In the back of Mandilé's mind lurks the fear of the uncertainties that may arise if the national team fails to deliver stellar performances. She understands the transient nature of coaching positions in the world of soccer, and a string of poor results could potentially jeopardize Kazimir's role and, consequently, their future together. She wishes for Kazimir's continued presence in Roshwari, not just for the success of the national team but also for the stability and growth of their relationship. She envisions a future where they can share both triumphs and challenges, and the success of the team becomes a crucial factor in realizing this vision. Caught in the delicate balance between personal desires and professional outcomes, Mandilé experiences heightened stress during each match. The weight of expectations, both for Kazimir's coaching career and the longevity of their relationship, presses heavily upon her shoulders.

Mandilé's emotional investment in Kazimir's coaching journey becomes evident in her reactions to the game's twists and turns. The ebb and flow of emotions mirror the highs and lows of the soccer matches, creating a parallel narrative of shared dreams and aspirations. Despite the stress, Mandilé remains a supportive presence, cheering on the national team with unwavering enthusiasm. Her hope is that Kazimir's coaching abilities will shine through, not only for the sake of victories on the field but for the victories they hope to achieve in their shared future.

## Navigating through the cultural expectations' influences

The struggles intensified as social beliefs clashed with the couple's desire for a life together. Mandilé's unwavering support from Linassa, Sandra, Saline, and Clara became a testament to the strength of friendship and the power of unity in the face of adversity. Each triumph on the soccer field paralleled the couple's journey of overcoming societal barriers, proving that love could endure, even against all odds. Mandilé already had opportunities to hear parents and extended family members' opinions about marrying a Muslim man already married. They are convinced that the difficulty Christian families may experience in accepting a Muslim man as a second husband for their daughter is often rooted in a combination of cultural, religious, and societal factors. For Riley (2015), It's important to note that individual attitudes and beliefs can vary widely, and not every Christian family would share the same concerns. There are many reasons that might contribute to the challenges. "Christianity and Islam are distinct religions with different beliefs and practices" (Riley, 2015). Mandilé's family is concerned about how the religious disparity will impact family life, including the upbringing of children in a mixed-faith household. Her brother explained that:

> *"In many societies, cultural norms play a significant role in shaping expectations around marriage. Marrying into a different cultural or religious background can be seen as deviating from established norms, leading to concerns about social acceptance and familial harmony. Some writers believe that "differences in religious practices, rituals, and traditions may raise concerns about potential discord within the family. Families may worry about how these differences could affect family celebrations, holidays, and daily routines". (Romano, 2016).*

Other authors consider that *"In some communities, there might be a social stigma associated with interfaith marriages. Families may fear judgment or ostracization from their social circle, community, or religious congregation"* (Van Beurden, 2013). For her, *"lack of understanding can be added as a challenge because misconceptions and stereotypes about different religious groups can contribute to apprehension"*.

This raises the problem of the nuances of each faith may lead to unfounded fears and reservations. How do you treat fairly each spouse? If Islam states it clearly, there is still a concern because introducing a second spouse, especially from a different faith, may raise concerns about fairness and equality among the family members. *"There may be worries about whether both spouses and their children will be treated equitably"*. (Stokes & Wright, 2000).

Mandilé now feels pressure from the extended family (grandmother, cousins) who try to exert influence on decisions related to marriage. They hold strong opinions and expectations, which create additional challenges for Mandilé and Kazimir. Nevertheless, Mandilé's mom did not have specific expectations for their children's marriages, including marrying within the same religious community.

The couple may not meet resistance from her.

Mandilé sits with her sister Linassa, visibly troubled. The room is adorned with warm colours, but Mandilé's dilemma casts a shadow over the atmosphere.

```
MANDILÉ
(teary-eyed)
"Linassa, I love Kazimir. I can't imagine my life without him, but
my family won't accept our relationship because he's Muslim."

LINASSA
(softly)
"I understand, Mandilé. Love can be a complicated journey."

MANDILÉ
(sighs)
"I want to be with him, but the pressure from our family is
overwhelming. They won't even consider the possibility of us being
together."

LINASSA
(nods)
"I've been through something similar, Mandilé. When I married a
foreigner, it wasn't well-received by our family initially. It
took time for them to come around."

MANDILÉ
(baffled)
"But Kazimir is such a good man. Why can't they see that?"
```

LINASSA
(smiles)
"Sometimes, it's not about the person but about the preconceived notions and prejudices. You have to decide what's more important — conforming to expectations or following your heart."

Mandilé wipes away her tears, contemplating Linassa's words.

MANDILÉ
"But what if they never accept us? I can't bear the thought of losing my family."

LINASSA
(earnestly)
"Mandilé, family is important, but so is your happiness. I faced the same dilemma, and yes, it was tough initially. But I stood by my decision, and eventually, they saw the love and happiness my husband brought into my life."

MANDILÉ
(resigned)
"I just don't want to lose them, Linassa."

LINASSA
(putting a hand on her shoulder)
"You won't lose them forever, Mandilé. Sometimes, they need time to understand that love knows no boundaries. Don't rush it, but don't sacrifice your happiness for the sake of conforming."

Mandilé looks at her sister, conflicted but grateful for the support.

MANDILÉ
"What if it takes too long? What if they never come around?"

LINASSA
(optimistic)
"Love is patient. Give them time. And who knows, maybe they'll surprise you."

The room falls into a thoughtful silence as Mandilé contemplates the difficult decision she faces – choosing between love and familial expectations.

# Chapter VIII: Success on the field, turmoil in the Heart

Kazimir and Mandilé found themselves in a perpetual dance between love and societal expectations. The whispers and judgmental glances echoed louder as their relationship endured. Their commitment to each other faced tests that only strengthened their resolve. Kazimir, torn between the success he achieved on the field and the persistent struggles in his personal life, began questioning the sacrifices required for a love that seemed destined to be marred by external forces.

Amidst the societal pressures, Mandilé's unwavering determination to be with Kazimir became the anchor that kept their love afloat. Linassa, Sandra, Saline, and Clara continued to stand by Mandilé's side, forming a formidable support system against the storm of cultural expectations.

The chapter unfolded with an air of uncertainty, yet the couple's love, though weathered, stood tall in the face of societal adversity.

With the past behind them, Kazimir and Mandilé faced new challenges that tested the endurance of their love. Society's judgments, the lingering echoes of past secrecy, and the natural ebb and flow of relationships became hurdles they had to overcome. Mandilé's friendship with Sandra evolved into a source of strength, proving that transparency and communication could mend even the deepest wounds.

Sandra, understanding the impact of their previous secrecy, became an advocate for open communication. The trio navigated through the complexities of love and friendship, learning that honesty, vulnerability, and mutual understanding were the pillars that sustained enduring relationships. As societal expectations continued to cast shadows, Kazimir, Mandilé, and friends stood united, challenging the norms that sought to dictate the course of their lives.

# Mandilé Family House – Sunday Lunch

## Mandilé's family house: a haven of tradition and warmth

Mandilé's family home stands as a symbol of stability, tradition, and familial warmth. Settled within a vibrant Roshwarian neighbourhood, 20mn away from Galida downtown, the house is a gracious three-bedroom residence that has witnessed the growth and shared experiences of Mandilé, her mother, and siblings, and the echoes of their familial bonds. The house, surrounded by a well-maintained garden, boasts a welcoming facade with vibrant flowers adorning the front. A sturdy and artistically designed gate provides both security and a touch of elegance to the property. The exterior reflects the pride the family takes in maintaining their home. Inside, the home exudes a sense of cosiness and comfort.

The living spaces are adorned with photographs capturing moments from Mandilé's childhood, family gatherings, and milestones. The living room serves as a central hub for shared conversations, laughter, and the creation of lasting memories. The four bedrooms are a testament to the individual personalities within the family. Mandilé's room, a reflection of her identity, features elements of both Roshwarian tradition and her Christian upbringing.

The other bedrooms, occupied by her siblings, each tell a unique story through personal decorations and cherished belongings.

Inherent in every corner of the house are traces of the family's strong Roshwarian traditional values. Decorative elements, family heirlooms, and religious symbols coexist harmoniously, creating an environment where the past and present seamlessly merge.

Mandilé and her siblings were raised within the walls of this home with a blend of strict Christian education and the rich cultural tapestry of Roshwarian traditions. The family home became a sanctuary where faith was nurtured, values were instilled, and the importance of community and connection was deeply ingrained.

The dining area and kitchen serve as communal spaces where the family comes together to share meals, discuss daily happenings, and reinforce the bonds that define them. The aroma of traditional Roshwarian (beans, potatoes, meat and green sleeves) dishes often wafts through the air, creating an atmosphere of familiarity and comfort.

## Sunday lunch's embarrassing atmosphere and the clash of faiths

Mandilé's family has set a warm and inviting table for Kazimir. The scent of home-cooked meals fills the air as Mandilé and Linassa eagerly await the arrival of their special guest. Mandilé's mother is absent due to illness, but her two brothers and a couple of cousins are present.

```
LINASSA
(smiling)
"I'm so excited for Coach Kazimir to join us. This lunch is going
to be amazing!"

MANDILÉ
```

(nervously)
"Yes, it's nice that he accepted the invitation. I hope everything goes well."

The doorbell rings, signalling Coach Kazimir's arrival. Mandilé answers the door with a welcoming smile.

KAZIMIR
(cheerfully)
"Thank you for having me. I hope your mother is feeling better soon."

MANDILÉ
(regretfully)
"She couldn't make it today, but she sends her regards."

The family gathers around the table, engaging in light-hearted conversation before the meal. However, the atmosphere takes an unexpected turn as Mandilé's brother subtly steers the conversation toward Coach Kazimir's beliefs.

As Mandilé's family prepares to gather for lunch, an atmosphere charged with religious differences hangs over the dining table. The air is thick with unspoken tension as Mandilé's family, deeply rooted in Christian traditions, extends an invitation for Kazimir, a devout Muslim, to join them in prayer before the meal. The dining table is adorned with a spread of Roshwarian delicacies, reflecting the family's culinary traditions. Plates filled with aromatic dishes are laid out, creating a tempting display that momentarily distracts from the underlying tension.

Mandilé's brother, a figure of authority and tradition in the household, extends a courteous yet somewhat awkward invitation to Kazimir. The invitation is accompanied by a subtle expectation that he partakes in the Christian prayer ritual before the meal.

As the family members exchange looks, there's an unspoken acknowledgement of the cultural and religious differences at play. Kazimir, though appreciative of the hospitality, senses the discomfort and internally grapples with the dilemma of adhering to his own religious practices. The room falls into an awkward silence as the family patiently waits for Kazimir's response. The clinking of cutlery and the ambient sounds of the household underscore the discomfort, amplifying the weight of the moment. Kazimir, respectful of the family's invitation, contemplates how to navigate this delicate situation. He understands the significance of the invitation, yet he also feels a responsibility to stay true to his own religious observances.

Linassa, caught in the middle, attempts to diffuse the tension by offering a warm smile and subtly gesturing towards the family's Christian artefacts. She seeks to bridge the gap and demonstrate cultural sensitivity, understanding the importance of both her family's Christian values and Kazimir's Muslim faith.

The diner's flow keeps on moving without Kazimir having the obligation to lead the prayer. Nevertheless, Mandilé's brother continues with another attempt to upset Kazimir.

```
MANDILÉ'S BROTHER
(raising an eyebrow)
"So, Coach Kazimir, what are your plans for the future?"

KAZIMIR
(smiling)
"Well, I'm focused on my coaching career and building meaningful
connections."

Mandilé's brother exchanges a knowing glance with the others, and
a plan unfolds.

MANDILÉ'S COUSIN
(suggestively)
"Speaking of connections, Mandilé is still a student, you know.
Marriage might be a bit premature; wouldn't you agree? And you are
```

a married Muslim, right?"

Coach Kazimir, sensing the orchestrated intervention, grows increasingly disappointed.

KAZIMIR
(confused)
"I appreciate your concern, but personal decisions are best made with understanding and mutual agreement."

MANDILÉ
(whispering to Linassa)
"What's happening? I didn't expect this."

LINASSA
(whispering back)
"I have no idea. This wasn't part of the plan."

As the family continues to subtly discourage the idea of Coach Kazimir and Mandilé being together, Coach Kazimir starts to feel uncomfortable and disappointed.

KAZIMIR
(polite but disappointed)
"I appreciate the concern, but I believe personal decisions should be made with open communication. Excuse me."

Coach Kazimir excuses himself from the table, leaving behind a puzzled Mandilé and Linassa.

MANDILÉ
(angry)
"What was that all about?"

LINASSA
(frustrated)
"I have no idea. Let's find out."

The two frustrated sisters confront the family members, demanding an explanation for the unexpected interference in their personal

lives. The family, realizing their mistake, watches as Coach
Kazimir leaves, understanding that their well-intentioned plan has
backfired.

Mandilé storms into the living room, her frustration is evident.
Linassa follows closely behind.

MANDILÉ
(angry)
"That was completely unfair! I can't believe you all did that
without even asking me."

MANDILÉ'S BROTHER
(defensive)
"We were just looking out for your future, Mandilé."

LINASSA
(firmly)
"By sabotaging her personal life? That's not looking out; that's
controlling."

Mandilé takes a deep breath, attempting to calm herself before
addressing her family.

MANDILÉ
(assertively)
"Listen, I love Coach Kazimir. He's providing everything,
including my school fees that you're so concerned about. He
respects me, and he's the one I want to be with."

MANDILÉ'S COUSIN
(concerned)
"But Mandilé, you need to focus on your studies."

MANDILÉ'
(emphatically)
"And I can do that with Coach Kazimir by my side. I won't let you
dictate my life."

Mandilé's words hang in the air, her family now realizing the

```
depth of her feelings and determination.

MANDILÉ'S BROTHER
(trying to justify)
"We just want what's best for you, Mandilé."

MANDILÉ
(fiercely)
"What's best for me is being with someone I love and who supports
me. If you can't accept that, then I'll make my own choices."

As Mandilé heads towards the door, Linassa stands by her side,
showing unwavering support.

LINASSA
(resolute)
"We're leaving. Mandilé deserves to make her own decisions."

MANDILÉ
(to the family)
"I'll plan my future with Coach Kazimir, with or without your
approval. Goodbye."
```

Mandilé and Linassa exit the family house, leaving behind a family in stunned silence. The weight of Mandilé's words lingers, and the family is left to reflect on their actions and the consequences of trying to control someone's happiness.

## Linassa's concern about the nonresistance attitude of Kazimir

Linassa, observing Coach Kazimir's non-resistance attitude in the face of family opposition to his decision to marry Mandilé, couldn't conceal her frustration. In a candid conversation with Kazimir, she expressed her disappointment and concern about his seemingly passive stance during family gatherings. Linassa, known for her straightforward nature, pointed out that a union as significant as marriage required assertiveness, especially when met with resistance. Her complaint revolved around Kazimir's reluctance to defend his project and articulate the reasons behind his choice. Linassa felt that Kazimir's non-confrontational approach, while perhaps reflective of his desire to avoid conflict, was hindering the clarity of his intentions. She emphasized the importance of him standing firm in the face of opposition, not only to assert the validity of his relationship with Mandilé but also to ensure that his commitment was communicated unequivocally to their families.

Linassa's concern stemmed from a belief that Kazimir's passivity might be interpreted as indecision or lack of commitment, potentially influencing the family's perception of the relationship. She encouraged Kazimir to find a balance between diplomacy and assertiveness, emphasizing that effective communication was key to fostering understanding and acceptance among family members.

Coach Kazimir, in response to Linassa's complaint about his non-confrontational attitude, shared a heartfelt explanation rooted in his understanding of the complex dynamics surrounding religious and cultural differences. He acknowledged the validity of Linassa's concerns while offering insights into his approach.

Kazimir began by expressing his deep respect for both his own cultural background and that of Mandilé. He explained that his non-confrontational stance was driven by a conscious effort to navigate the sensitive terrain of religious and cultural differences without inadvertently causing strife within the family. He emphasized that, for him, the goal was not to challenge or change anyone's beliefs but rather to foster understanding and acceptance.

The coach highlighted the inherent challenges in convincing people to shift their deeply ingrained beliefs, especially when it came to matters as personal and profound as religion. He explained that, instead of engaging in confrontations that could potentially deepen divides, he chose a more diplomatic approach. Kazimir conveyed his belief that actions, over time, would speak louder than words, and through his consistent love and commitment to Mandilé, he hoped to gradually shift perspectives.

In essence, Kazimir's explanation centred on the recognition that change often takes time and that a confrontational approach might not be the most effective strategy when dealing with matters of faith and tradition. His intention was to lead by example, demonstrating through his actions the strength and sincerity of his love for Mandilé while allowing the family the space to evolve in their understanding over time.

## Saline and Clara's perspectives on religion and traditions

After leaving the family Sunday meeting with a heavy heart, Mandilé sought consolation in the company of her friends, Saline and Clara. Lay in a comfy corner of their favourite hangout spot, the trio engaged in a candid conversation that delved into their diverse perspectives on religion and traditions.

Saline and Clara, both firm in their beliefs, shared a common scepticism toward organized religions. Their view was rooted in the belief that religions were constructs designed by people to exert control, particularly in African societies where religious matters often overshadow socio-economic development. For them, traditions held value, but they emphasized the importance of personal growth and fulfilment above all.

As they sipped on their drinks, Mandilé listened attentively to her friends' perspectives. Saline, with her pragmatic approach, argued that adherence to traditions should not hinder individual achievement, highlighting the need for a balance between cultural practices and personal aspirations. Clara, on the other hand, expressed her disdain for the institutionalization of religious practices, advocating for a more nuanced understanding of spirituality that aligns with personal goals.

Mandilé, caught in the crossroads of love, cultural expectations, and personal beliefs, found comfort in the non-judgmental space her friends provided. The conversation illuminated the contrasting worldviews that coexisted within their circle, demonstrating the complexity of navigating faith, traditions, and individual aspirations in a changing society. This encounter with Saline and Clara became a crucial moment of introspection for Mandilé, challenging her to reconcile her own beliefs and desires in the midst of societal expectations.

While the specific positions of Saline and Clara are reflective of personal beliefs and societal observations, their perspectives resonate with broader discussions on religion, tradition, and personal development. This led Mandilé to activate her curiosity and start doing research. She found out that Saline and Clara's viewpoints have been supported by Richard Dawkins who *"challenges traditional views on religion and explores the idea that organized religions may have been constructed to control societies. He provides a critical examination of religious beliefs and their impact on individuals and societies".* (Dawkins, 2011).

In another approach, Harari (2015), explores the evolution of human societies, including the role of religion and traditions. It offers a perspective on how cultural constructs, including religious beliefs, have shaped human history. For him, *"it is axiomatic that a personal God or the gods do not exist as metaphysical entities, though he confesses an openness to contemplating the 'mystery of existence".* He sees religions as *"imagined orders, because they offer rules that tell people how to cooperate, and they're based on a "belief" in something beyond the physical world".* (Harari, 2015).

Some of these views faced challenges and criticism, especially with Harris (2004) whose remark on the dangers of religious dogma and the idea that faith can be a hindrance to social progress, have been criticized by Anab Whitehouse, a Muslim writer. He believes that:

> *"The irony that resides at the core of books like The End of Faith — along with books such as The God Delusion, by Richard Dawkins, and God is*

*not Great by Christopher Hitchens — is that while each of the authors of these books purports to be a rationalist, all too frequently, **reason** seems to be absent from their respective modes of thinking. At least this appears to be so when considered in the context of issues concerning God's existence".* (*Whitehouse, 2018*).

This fight between scholars won't help Mandilé in her quest for truth, it brings another perspective to her already so confused opinion despite Saline and Clara's supportive ideas. Instead, she decided to focus on her love, knowing, without reasoning, that love is unfocused. And without love, reasoning is impersonal, even sometimes inhuman. *"Love often seems dramatically unreasonable, and reason can seem coldly rational in a way that excludes any emotion, passion, or affiliation"* (Bialek, 2023)

# Chapter IX: Beyond the Goalposts

A s Kazimir and Mandilé stood united, their love transcended the boundaries set by culture and tradition. The couple faced an uncertain future, but their love, resilience, and the lessons learned on the field and in life remained eternally intertwined. This chapter invites readers to contemplate the power of love and the resilience required to defy societal norms. Kazimir and Mandilé's journey became a testament to the enduring strength of the human spirit and the possibility of finding love beyond the goalposts.

## Defying Societal Norms: The Power of Time and Love

Societal norms often dictate the expected path of individuals, influencing decisions regarding relationships, careers, and personal aspirations. However, the enduring forces of time and love have the capacity to challenge and overcome these norms, ushering in transformative change.

Time is a catalyst for change because over time, societies evolve, and perspectives shift. What may have been considered unconventional or unacceptable in the past can gradually become more accepted and normalized. As generations change, so do societal attitudes, making room for diverse expressions of love and life choices. Love, with its transformative and boundary-defying nature, has the power to challenge societal norms.

When individuals genuinely love each other, regardless of societal expectations or prejudices, they often find the strength to confront and challenge those norms, paving the way for a more inclusive and understanding society. The passage of time allows for the breaking down of generational barriers. Younger generations, exposed to diverse perspectives and ideas, often challenge and redefine societal norms. Love, especially when it transcends traditional boundaries, becomes a catalyst for generational shifts, fostering a more open-minded and accepting society. With time, education becomes a powerful tool in challenging societal norms. As individuals gain access to knowledge and diverse experiences, they are better equipped to question and challenge established norms. Love, supported by informed choices, becomes a driving force in breaking away from restrictive societal expectations.

Even cultures evolve over time, and love plays a crucial role in this evolution. As people from different backgrounds come together in love, cultural exchange occurs, challenging rigid norms and fostering a more inclusive society that embraces diversity. Time allows for the gradual acceptance and integration of these changes into the cultural fabric. Indeed, time allows for the reevaluation of societal expectations in relationships. As love stories unfold that defy traditional norms, they become narratives that challenge and reshape societal perceptions. Over time, these stories contribute to a broader understanding of love and relationships, fostering acceptance and inclusivity. To be short, the interplay of time and love holds the potential to defy and conquer societal norms. Kazimir and Mandilé's case teaches us that, as societies evolve, driven by the transformative power of love, individuals find the strength to challenge existing expectations and contribute to a more accepting, diverse, and inclusive world.

# "Love's triumph and chaos: Coach kazimir's proposal and the unspoken confrontation"

In a pivotal moment, Coach Kazimir, consumed by the depth of his love for Mandilé, took the courageous decision to propose to her, envisioning a future filled with shared dreams and aspirations. As he knelt before Mandilé, he felt a mix of joy and trepidation, knowing that this union would not come without its challenges. The gravity of his choice sank in as he contemplated the difficult conversation, he needed to have with his current wife, Saran, left behind in Sangouna.

The prospect of facing the emotional turmoil that awaited him left Coach Kazimir caught in the whirlwind of conflicting emotions—happiness for the prospect of a life with Mandilé and the weight of the impending conversation that would alter the course of his relationships. Amidst the joy of newfound love, a cloud of uncertainty and the responsibility of addressing the consequences of his decisions cast a poignant shadow on Coach Kazimir's heart. As the battle against societal norms ends, another chapter of struggle is pending.

In the looming weeks before Coach Kazimir's return to Sangouna, the weight of the impending announcement to his current wife presses heavily on his shoulders. Torn between the happiness he envisions with Mandilé and the moral obligation to be honest with his present spouse, Coach Kazimir finds solace in the counsel of a trusted friend. Seeking advice becomes a therapeutic outlet, a means to navigate the complex emotions and ethical dilemmas that cloud his mind.

Coach Kazimir grappling with the realization that his decisions will not only redefine his own life but will also have profound repercussions on the lives of those entwined with his. The narrative hints at the complexity of human relationships, the delicate dance between love, duty, and the inevitability of facing the consequences of one's choices. As Coach Kazimir prepares to embark on a journey back to Sangouna, many questions are raised in his head. Will he keep his promises to Mandilé as he proposed to her already? Will the wedding plan not be jeopardized by the outcome of his meeting with his wife? Is Mandilé's family still in a resistance mode regarding the marriage? Let's be prepared to be left on the precipice of an emotional climax, eagerly anticipating the resolution of his inner chaos.

# Conclusion

I n these chapters of "Beyond the Whistle," the story takes a daring turn as Kazimir, the successful soccer coach, has already proposed to Mandilé, defying societal expectations and the resistance embedded in cultural norms. The culmination of their love story unfolds against the backdrop of Roshwari's beautiful landscapes and the complexities of intercultural relationships. As Kazimir stands at the crossroads of his personal life, having achieved remarkable success with the national soccer team, he faces a new challenge that transcends the soccer pitch. Proposing to Mandilé is not merely a declaration of love; it is a courageous act that challenges prevailing social norms and religious expectations.

However, the journey towards matrimonial bliss is far from over. Kazimir, committed to transparency and honesty, must now navigate the delicate task of convincing his wife, Saran, left behind in Sangouna, about his intention to take a second wife. The hurdles he encounters reflect the intricate dance between love, culture, and faith.

The storyline intricately weaves together the threads of personal conviction, societal pressures, and the resilience of love. Kazimir's pursuit of happiness unfolds not only on the soccer field but within the intricate tapestry of relationships, testing the boundaries of tradition and introducing readers to the complex dynamics of polygamous marriages.

"Beyond the Whistle" leaves the door open for a continuation, inviting readers to explore the unfolding chapters of Kazimir and Mandilé's journey. Will Kazimir successfully navigate the complexities of polygamy and find acceptance in both his marriages? How will Mandilé cope with societal expectations and the challenges that lie ahead? The narrative hints at the potential for a sequel, where love, cultural clashes, and faith intersect in the ongoing saga of Kazimir's life. As you reflect on the ultimate pages of "Beyond the Whistle," I am sure are left with a sense of anticipation, eager to embark on the next chapter of Kazimir and Mandilé's unconventional love story. This is not an endpoint but a transition, inviting you to accompany the characters on their continued journey through the intricacies of love and life.

# Afterword

⸎

# Beyond the Whistle: A Coach Love Story

*"Love Knows No Boundaries"*

In the heart of Roshwari, where the echoes of a coach's whistle carry the promise of passion and the challenge of tradition, unfolds a tale that transcends the ordinary. "Beyond the Whistle" invites you to witness the captivating journey of Coach Kazimir, whose life becomes intricately woven with the enchanting Mandilé. As love blossoms amidst the cultural tapestry of Roshwari, this fiction navigates the delicate dance between tradition and personal aspirations. The red rose, symbolizing love and drama, graces the cover, setting the stage for a narrative that explores the complexities of relationships and the clash of diverse cultures.

Key Themes: Love that defies conventions

*Why Read "Beyond the Whistle"?*

This novel is more than a love story; it's an exploration of the human experience in the face of love, drama, and cultural diversity. With each chapter, the author skillfully unfolds a captivating narrative that challenges preconceived notions and invites readers to reflect on their own journey through life's complexities.

# Bibliography

Bialek. (2023). Love and reason. Saint Louis, Washington: Washington University, Arts and Sciences, Religious Studies.

Dawkins, R. (2011). *The God Delusion.* Harpercollins.

Harari, Y. N. (2015). *Sapiens: A Brief History of Humankind.* HarperCollins.

Racco, M. (2017, December 14). *How to manage differences in religious beliefs in a relationship.* Retrieved from Global News, Lifestyle: https://globalnews.c a/news/3905900/religion-in-relationships/

Riley, N. S. (2015). Interfaith Marriage in America: Patterns and Trends. *Journal of Religion and Society.*

Romano, D. (2016). Intercultural Marriage: Promises and Pitfalls. *Routledge.*

Srivastava, N. (2020, 06 7). *Bruce Lee: "Mistakes are always forgivable if one has the courage to admit them.".* Retrieved from Yoga Anatomy Pilates: https://www.yoga-anatomy.com/bruce-lee-mistakes-are-always-forgivable-if-one-has-the-courage-to-admit-them

Stokes, C., & Wright, E. (2000). Religious Intermarriage in the United States: Determinants and Trends. *Social Science Research.*

Van Beurden, S. (2013). Religious Interfaith Marriages in Comparative Perspective: The Case of Dutch-Moroccan and Dutch-Turkish Muslims. *Journal of Muslims in Europe.*

Whitehouse, A. (2018). *Sam Harris and the End of Faith: A Critique.* Brewer, Main.

Wicker, P., Breuer, C., & Schröder, D. P. (2016). social Cohesion through

Football: A Multinational Case Study. *European Sport Management Quarterly.*
Zafar, I. (2020, September 10). *Embracing Forgiveness.* Retrieved from
Readers blog: https://timesofindia.indiatimes.com/readersblog/zafarreads/
embracing-forgiveness-25820/#

# About the Author

Dr Cheikh Sarr (PhD) is a skilled storyteller who weaves narratives that resonate with the human spirit. With a keen understanding of diverse cultures and a passion for exploring the complexities of relationships, the author invites readers to delve into the rich tapestry of "Beyond the Whistle."

He was born in Joal Fadiouth and spent his entire youth in Thiès (Senegal) where he obtained his BAC at the Malick Sy High School. He continued his university studies at INSEPS of Dakar where he obtained his 6 years' CAPEPS diploma. He was certified in Sports Psychology from Germany in 2003 before joining the University of Delaware (USA) where he obtained his master's degree in Education and Sports Management in 2008. After 3 years as director of SEEDS Academy, his passion for studies and research encouraged his engagement as a teacher-researcher at Gaston Berger University in 2011 where he obtained his Doctorate in Sports Psychology in 2016. Throughout his course, he merged studies and Basketball. The numerous national and international competitions in which he participated as a national coach earned him a reputation as a rigorous and hardworking man. Her results during the men's (2014) and women's (2018) World Cups have given her worldwide recognition. Today, his status as instructor of instructors at the FIBA World Association of Coaches (WABC) rings like a consecration, hence the numerous training courses, clinics and camps carried out in several cities (Abidjan, Antananarivo, Antsirabe, Bujumbura, Douala, Dubai, Garoua, Johannesburg, Kigali, Man, Musanzé, Port Elisabeth, Porto-Novo, St Louis, etc.

Discover a captivating fiction that goes beyond the ordinary. Get your copy of "Beyond the Whistle" and embark on a journey where love takes centre stage, and the drama unfolds in unexpected ways.

**You can connect with me on:**

𝕏 https://twitter.com/coachcheikh

f https://web.facebook.com/cdiokhsarr

ℰ https://www.instagram.com/cheikh68

ℰ https://www.linkedin.com/in/dr-cheikh-sarr-03b17779

# Also by Cheikh SARR

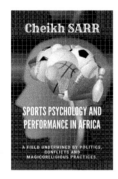

**Cheikh SARR**

SPORTS PSYCHOLOGY AND
PERFORMANCE IN AFRICA

A FIELD UNDERMINED BY POLITICS,
CONFLICTS AND
MAGICORELIGIOUS PRACTICES

**Sports Psychology and Performance in Africa: A Field Undermined by Politics, Conflicts and Magicoreligious Practices.**

The book *"Sports Psychology and Performance in Africa"* addresses a crucial question: does winning or losing depend on the abilities of a marabout? This question is particularly challenging as it delves into the integration of sports psychology, a scientific discipline, into an African sports environment already entrenched with mystical practices. Many athletes perceive the impact of these practices on performance as real, complicating the introduction of sports psychology.

However, some sports organizations view mystical practices negatively, conflicting with their values of fair play and neutrality toward players' personal beliefs. Despite this challenge, there is an optimistic perspective.

The book caters to sports science students, offering a comprehensive resource covering key concepts, theories, and practical applications in sports psychology. It goes beyond conventional classroom use, serving as a foundational text for online resources, multimedia content, or interactive exercises, enhancing the overall learning experience.

*"Sports Psychology and Performance in Africa"* explores the hidden aspects of sports, exploring its connections with violence, media, racism, doping, studies, and religion. This approach reflects a coherent educational strategy.

The book takes a critical stance on sports psychology within the broader African context. It analyzes the legitimization of psychosociological and magico-religious practices in modern sports at the expense of sports psychology. The latter, being relatively new in Africa, faces obstacles such as limited acceptance by athletes and sports organizations.

African athletes may prioritize physical over mental aspects of training due

84

to a lack of awareness or education regarding sports psychology's benefits. Additionally, limited financial and human resources hinder the discipline's development in Africa.

While sports organizations in Africa consider mystical practices effective for influencing performance, some view them negatively, conflicting with professional values of fair play and neutrality.

The book's second aim is to unveil contradictions and hidden interests in societal and organizational discourses on sports. It explores the dual nature of sports, where some emphasize its values, while others see it as a reflection of a society influenced by politics, religion, racism, media, and violence.

In short, the book navigates the intricate relationship between sports psychology and mystical practices in Africa, addressing challenges, providing educational resources, and critically analyzing the broader societal and organizational dynamics of sports.